Destiny
the Pop Star Fairy

Daisy Meadows

ORCHARD

www.rainbowmagicbooks.co.uk

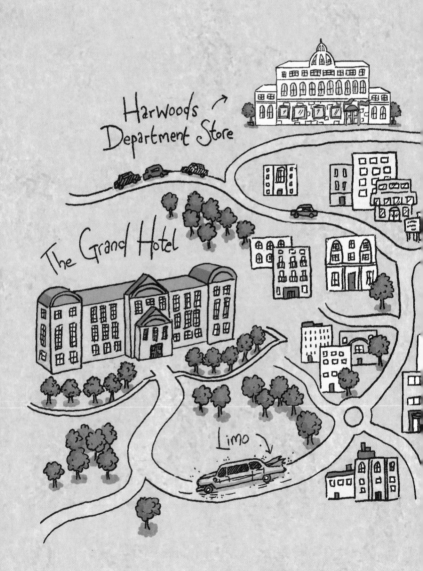

Harwoods
Department Store

The Grand Hotel

Limo

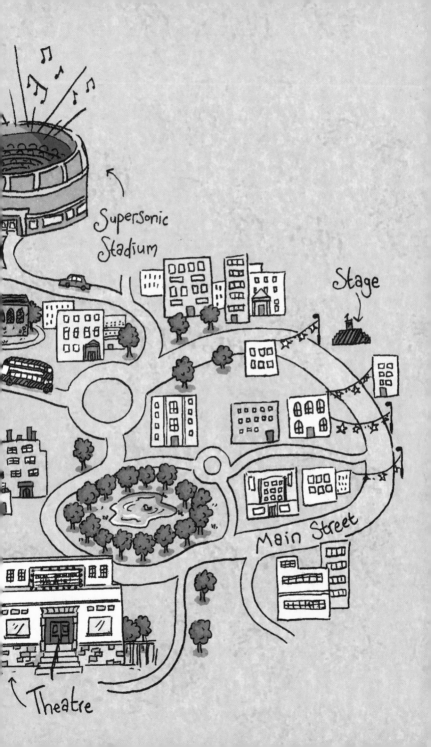

Contents

Story One:

The Sparkle Sash   9

Story Two:

The Keepsake Key   31

Story Three:

The Magical Microphone   55

Story One

The Sparkle Sash

The Sparkle Sash

"I can't believe we're really going to meet Serena, Emilia and Lexy!" said Kirsty Tate to her best friend Rachel Walker. The girls had won a competition to meet their favourite band, The Angels.

The girls were staying overnight with their parents at The Grand Hotel before helping the band turn on the city's Christmas lights, and attending a charity concert. "This is almost as exciting as one of our fairy adventures!" Rachel whispered to her best friend. No one else knew that they had a special friendship with the fairies.

"Oh, Rachel, look!" cried Kirsty. On a table in a corner of their room was a huge bunch of flowers, with a handwritten card on top. It was from the girls in the band!

Dear Kirsty and Rachel,
We hope you have a fun stay! We are really looking forward to meeting you later today. Serena, Emilia & Lexy
— The Angels xxx

"Look at the Christmas tree!" cried Rachel, as they explored their enormous suite. As she spoke, there was a burst of glitter, and a beautiful fairy appeared.

"Hello," she began in a tinkling voice. "I'm Destiny the Pop Star Fairy, and I need your help."

The delighted but startled girls waited for her to explain.

"I look after pop stars in the human world and Fairyland," she began. "Jack Frost wants to perform at our Christmas concert with his group, but their audition was awful! Now he's so cross he says he'll rid the world of pop music completely!"

"How could Jack Frost get rid of all music?" asked a horrified Kirsty.

"I have three magical

objects," sighed the tiny fairy. "The Sparkle Sash protects pop stars' outfits and costumes. The Keepsake Key protects their songs and music, and the Magical Microphone ensures the sound and lighting work smoothly." The girls listened as

Destiny continued.

"Jack Frost has stolen them, and ordered his goblins to hide them. He wants to spoil The Angels' Christmas concert at the same time."

"But that's tomorrow!" gasped Kirsty. "What can we do to help?"

"Stay alert," said Destiny. "The goblins are bound to cause trouble sooner or later."

It was time for the girls to head for the stadium, and all thoughts of Jack Frost and goblins flew from their minds. They were about to meet The Angels! Arriving at the stage door, the girls were led to the band's dressing room. The door opened, and The Angels rushed

over to hug them.

"Congratulations on winning the competition!" Serena said with a smile.

"It's great to meet you!" Lexy added, her copper-coloured

ringlets bouncing.

"You're going to get star treatment from our own stylists," Emilia told them. "But first we're going to teach you the dance routine for our brand-new song!"

Rachel and Kirsty were giggling with The Angels like old friends as the door opened. "Girls, meet Rich and Charlotte, our stylist and make-up artist," said Emilia. As Charlotte dabbed glitter onto their cheeks and eyelids, and Rich talked about what clothes would suit them, Emilia's mobile phone began to ring. Her face fell as soon as she answered it. "But this could ruin the whole show!" she cried. Rachel and Kirsty exchanged worried looks. Could this have something to do with Jack Frost? Emilia ended the call.

"The lorry carrying our costumes hasn't turned up!" she explained.

As everyone began talking at once, the girls slipped into the corridor. A little way down,

a storage room door was open.
"Oh, no!" said Kirsty,
stepping inside.
The room
was a mess.
Shimmering
costumes
were
smeared
with
purples, blues
and golds and
someone had used red
lipstick to draw a picture of
Jack Frost on the wall!

"Goblins!" muttered Kirsty crossly.

Suddenly a jet of glitter shot from the top of a silver boot, and Destiny appeared.

"We must find the Sparkle Sash before the goblins cause any more trouble!" she said, waving her wand and clearing the room in a flurry of magical sparkles.

The friends followed a horrible screeching sound to the stage, where the goblins were all dressed up and trying

 to sing.

"Look!" Kirsty exclaimed, pointing to something shimmery tied around the smallest goblin's waist.

"It's the Sparkle Sash!" Destiny exclaimed. "But how can we get it?"

"Let's teach them The Angels' dance routine!" smiled Kirsty. "Then you take the sash!"

Amid the chaos of clumsily

dancing goblins, Destiny managed to untie the sash. She returned it to  fairy size, and flitted away.

"Carry on practising!" Kirsty called out, running off the stage.

"They've stolen my sash!" shrieked the goblin furiously.

The disappointed goblins shuffled off towards the exit as Destiny waved her wand to clear up the stage. "Thank you so much for your help, girls," she said. "I could never have got this back without you."

"Are you going to take the sash back to Fairyland now?" asked Kirsty.

Destiny nodded.

"The sooner it's back in its rightful place, the better!" she declared.

Rachel and Kirsty waved as Destiny disappeared in a whirl of sparkles. "Come on," whispered Rachel. "Let's get back to The Angels!"

In the dressing room, Rachel and Kirsty found The Angels hugging and jumping around in excitement. "The lorry has been found!" Lexy squealed happily. "The driver's satnav sent him the  wrong way, then the lorry broke down, then his mobile battery ran out. But just then a breakdown truck rescued him, and his satnav started working again. Can you believe it?"

"Isn't it amazing that the truck was found so quickly, and then found its way here?" said Serena to the girls.

"It's like magic!" agreed Kirsty, winking at Rachel.

Now there were only two more magical objects left to find!

Story Two

The Keepsake Key

The Keepsake Key

Next morning, Mr Tate had a surprise for the girls. "We thought you'd like new outfits for the concert, so we're taking you to Harwoods," he smiled.

"Wow!" gasped Rachel. "The most famous department store in the city!"

While the adults chatted, Kirsty whispered in Rachel's ear. "What about the Keepsake Key? I really want to visit Harwoods, but we must help Destiny get her other two magical objects back. Jack Frost and his goblins can't be allowed to ruin pop music forever!" But before there was time to think, the girls were whisked off on their shopping trip.

Inside the magnificent store, Rachel and Kirsty travelled up the long escalators, feeling very excited. The fashion department was huge. As their parents wandered around, the girls hurried eagerly towards a rack of colourful sparkly clothes.

"Perfect!" said Rachel suddenly, holding up a pretty red skirt and distracting Kirsty. "This would look great on you!"

"And this would be just right for you," replied Kirsty, pulling out a pair of jeans with a sequin trim.

Suddenly a group of children in hooded tops pushed past them. "Hey," cried Kirsty. "Be careful!"

"It's odd to see children on their own," said Rachel thoughtfully, walking into the changing rooms.

The girls tried on their outfits, and as they were

putting on their own clothes again, Kirsty froze. Poking out from the bottom of the next cubicle was a pair of green feet!

"Now that is definitely a goblin!" Rachel hissed, pulling open the curtain. At first the

goblin inside
didn't
notice.
He was
wearing
a purple
suit and
a striped
waistcoat.
As the girls
watched, he raised his
hat and admired himself in the
mirror. Kirsty and Rachel burst
out laughing and watched the
goblin's green cheeks turn red.

"You horrible girls!" he stammered. "How dare you laugh at me!" He stuck his tongue out at them and shot off in a rage. The girls hurried after him, but ran straight into their parents, who were waiting outside.

"Now, let's look at the shoes," said Mrs Tate, smiling.

Rachel and Kirsty would

have to give up the chase for now.

As they headed up to the next floor on the escalator, the girls spotted three small figures wearing wigs running up and down, laughing and getting in

everyone's way.

"What's going on?" a security guard suddenly demanded.

"Run!" shrieked a figure in a blonde wig, as he led the others towards the music department.

The girls chose their shoes quickly, then asked if they could look round on their own.

"All right," said Mrs Walker. "We'll meet you in the café."

As the girls headed off, Rachel noticed a mirror tucked away in a quiet corner,

fizzing and
sparkling.
As she
peered
into it, a
small figure

burst through. It was
Destiny! She smiled as she
waved her wand and shrank
the girls to fairy size.

"Follow me!" she said
urgently, flying towards the
electrical department. With
another sparkling wave of her
wand, The Angels appeared on

every TV screen, sitting in their dressing room looking glum.

The girls looked confused as Destiny explained. "The Keepsake Key protects pop stars' songs. Every copy of the music for The Angels' new song has been stolen, and they've got to sing it tonight!"

"We're not going to let Jack Frost spoil everything," said Kirsty in a determined tone. "Come on, let's find those goblins and make them give back the Keepsake Key!"

When they reached the
music department, everything
seemed calm and quiet.

"Maybe they've gone," Rachel
suggested.

"No – listen!" said Kirsty.
The girls could hear a

squeaking sound which grew
louder and louder, until around
the corner sped a unicycle with
a squeaky wheel, ridden by
a goblin in a long silky dress.
Behind him was another on a
pogo stick wearing pyjamas,
and a third wobbling along on
roller blades.

"Look at what that goblin
on the pogo stick has around
his neck," Destiny said, tingling
with excitement. "It's my
Keepsake Key!"

"I think I can unfasten it and

fly away," Rachel whispered,
ducking behind the goblin's
shoulders and fluttering her
wings as she tried to undo the
chain.

"Something's tickling my
neck!" whined the
goblin, whirling
around and
spotting
Rachel.
"Look! A
fairy is trying
to steal the key!"
He yanked the

chain from around his neck
and tucked it into his pyjama
pocket.

"Run!" bellowed the
goblin on roller blades, as
they zoomed into the toy
department.

There were children
everywhere, but suddenly the
girls heard a familiar shriek.

"Look!" Rachel exclaimed
as they saw the three goblins
staring in fear at a guide dog.

"Silly goblins!" said Rachel.
"Guide dogs are the gentlest

dogs in the world!"

Destiny giggled, but Kirsty was looking thoughtful. "Did you see those battery-powered dogs?" she whispered, smiling. "Perhaps we can distract the goblins with them!"

"That's a great idea!" smiled Destiny. She used magic to create a cloud of colourful balloons to distract the children, while the girls flitted around, shepherding the goblins closer and closer to the yapping toy dogs.

"Eeek!" the goblins squealed. "Look at the hairy monsters! Help!"

"Goblins!" said Destiny,  fluttering above them. "Please return the Keepsake Key."

"No!"

squeaked the smallest goblin rudely.

At that moment one of the toy dogs yapped loudly, flipped over and landed in the lap of the goblin with the Keepsake Key. He screamed in terror, pulled the key from his pocket and threw it to Destiny, who shrank it to fairy size, catching it neatly.

"Thank you," she said, rising high into the air. "And by the way, those 'monsters' are just toys!"

"What?" roared the smallest goblin. "You tricksy fairies!"

Destiny and the girls fluttered back into the electrical department. "Thank you," the little fairy said. "I have to take the key to Fairyland but I'll be back soon. We still have to find the Magical Microphone!"

Destiny returned the girls to

human size, then disappeared in a shower of glitter.

A second later, The Angels appeared on the TV screens again, laughing this time. "Our song!" laughed Emilia, waving their sheet music around. "Our music's been found!"

Soon, the Christmas lights were due to be switched on. Then it would be time for the concert. Just one more magical object to find!

Story Three

The Magical Microphone

The Magical Microphone

Rachel and Kirsty quickly changed, ready for the switching on of the Christmas lights and the concert.

"Come on, girls!" called Mrs Tate, and a few seconds later, the two families hurried down to the hotel lobby.

Their parents left the hotel to make their own way, while the girls rushed over to The Angels, who were waiting for them in the lobby.

"Girls, you look great!" said Serena, giving them each a hug.

"Come on, our car's here!" They led the girls out of

the hotel. A long, pink Cadillac was waiting for them, with a smart chauffeur at the wheel. Jumping in with The Angels, Rachel and Kirsty felt like pop stars themselves!

"We're really excited about turning on the lights," Emilia told them. "It's such a special occasion."

As they set off, Serena pointed at a scooter riding alongside them in the traffic. Kirsty and Rachel looked out of the window and saw six goblins standing on the back of it in a pyramid shape.

"Oh no!" groaned Kirsty in a low voice. "Rachel, look at the driver!" It was Jack Frost!

"He's got the Magical Microphone!" whispered Rachel in Kirsty's ear.

As they watched, Jack Frost roared away. The goblins held on until suddenly, the goblin at the top began to wobble and lost his balance. He fell off the scooter and landed in the middle of the road!

"Luckily everyone's wearing fancy dress for the ceremony," whispered Kirsty. "People will think he's in a costume." The girls watched as the goblin leapt to his feet, and disappeared into the crowd.

Suddenly their car began to rattle, and then stopped.

"That's not good," said Lexy as the chauffeur and The Angels got out to see what was wrong.

"Kirsty, look!" Rachel cried in excitement. The gear stick was glowing and there, on the top of it, was Destiny!

"Destiny, Jack Frost is here in the human world and we can't follow him!" Kirsty blurted out,

almost before the little fairy
could speak.

Destiny waved her wand and
the car roared into life.

"The car broke down
because the Magical

Microphone is missing," Destiny explained. "It keeps all technical things around pop stars running smoothly."

Looking relieved, The Angels and the chauffeur jumped back into the car as Destiny dived into Rachel's handbag. They arrived at the podium with seconds to spare.

Rachel and Kirsty scanned the crowd, searching for Jack Frost.

"We are thrilled," Serena said to the crowd, "to be turning on

the Christmas lights this year."

As the girls were about to
press the button, Kirsty gripped
Rachel's hand. "I see him!" she
exclaimed excitedly.

Jack Frost was standing at the edge of the crowd. Before the girls could think what to do, he stuck out his tongue, then tapped his wand  against the Magical Microphone. All the lights went

out, leaving Main Street in
darkness. The crowd gasped.

Destiny quickly flew out of
Rachel's bag. The girls didn't
see her wave her wand, but
felt themselves shrinking to
fairy size. They all held hands
together and rose into the air.
The lights in the side streets
were still on, and almost at
once Rachel spotted a green
leg disappearing through the
side door of the theatre.

"This way!" she cried. Inside,
the lights were down and a

musical was in full swing. They
split up and began to search the
theatre. Luckily it was dark and
everyone was looking at the
stage. Kirsty grabbed the others'
hands and pointed. Jack Frost
was sitting in the back row
with five goblins. They were

making so much noise that they were disturbing everyone around them.

"They haven't seen us," said Kirsty. "Let's creep up and try to find the Magical Microphone."

"Boo!" shouted Jack Frost rudely.

"Rubbish!" shouted one of the goblins.

"They're spoiling the show for everyone!" cried Destiny.

Someone had obviously complained because just then

some stewards arrived and pinned Jack Frost's arms to his side.

"Lemme go!" wailed a goblin as another steward seized him by the shoulders.

"I don't care how much effort you've put into these silly costumes," hissed the chief steward furiously. "We're not putting up with this noise any longer."

Jack Frost and the goblins were hauled off and thrown out of the building. Rachel quickly flew over to where they had been, and found the Magical Microphone under Jack Frost's seat! Destiny waved her wand

and returned it to Fairyland size.

A minute later, the three friends landed back on the

podium in Main Street, next to The Angels.

"Thank you so much!" said Destiny happily. "Now I must

rush to Fairyland with the Magical Microphone!" And with a sprinkle of fairy dust, she returned the girls to their normal size.

"Happy Christmas, everyone!" shouted The Angels, Rachel and Kirsty as they pressed the big red button together. The lights flashed on, and the crowd cheered.

The concert that evening was spectacular, and at the end, Rachel and Kirsty went backstage

to say goodbye to The Angels
and thank them.

"I'm so sleepy!" yawned
Rachel as they changed into
their pyjamas in the hotel
room. "Oh, Kirsty – look!"

On each of their pillows was
a silver
mirror,
and on
the back
of each
was an
inscription
that said,

"With love and thanks, Destiny xx". When they looked into the glass, they could see her waving at them, with King Oberon and Queen Titania behind her.

"Thank you, and goodnight, everyone!" Rachel whispered. "See you again soon!"

The girls snuggled down into their beds.

"We've had lots of exciting adventures," murmured Kirsty. "But this has been the most star-studded one yet!"

**If you enjoyed this story,
you may want to read**

Keira the Film Star Fairy
Early Reader

Here's how the story begins...

"Look, there's Julianna
Stewart!" whispered Kirsty Tate.
"Isn't her fairy princess costume
beautiful?"

Rachel Walker peeked round
just as Julianna walked past.
The film star gave the girls a
friendly wink, then sat down
in a director's chair with her

name on the back to study her
script.

"Who'd have thought a really
famous actress like Julianna
would come to Wetherbury
village?" said Rachel.

"And who'd have thought
that she'd be spending most
of the school holidays in Mrs
Croft's garden?" added Kirsty.

Mrs Croft was a friend of
Kirsty's parents, a sweet old lady
who had lived in Wetherbury
for years. Her little thatched
cottage with pretty, blossoming

trees at the front often caught the eyes of tourists and passers-by. A few weeks ago when Mrs Croft had been working in her garden, an executive from a big film studio had pulled up outside. He wanted to book the cottage for a brand new film starring the famous actress Julianna Stewart. When Mrs Croft agreed, she became the talk of the village! Truckloads of set designers, lighting engineers and prop-makers had turned up to transform her garden into a magical world. Now filming on The Starlight Chronicles was about to begin.

"It was so kind of Mrs Croft to let us spend some time on set," said Rachel, watching the director talk through the next scene with his star.

Read
Keira the Film Star Fairy
Early Reader
to find out
what happens next!

Learn to read with

RAINBOW magic™

- Rainbow Magic Early Readers are easy-to-read versions of the original books

- Specially developed in conjunction with an early years Reading Consultant

- Perfect for parents to read aloud and for newly confident readers to read along

- Remember to enjoy reading together. It's never too early to share a story!

Everybody loves Daisy Meadows!

'I love your books' – Jasmine, Essex

'You are my favourite author' – Aimee, Surrey

'I am a big fan of Rainbow Magic!' – Emma, Hertfordshire

Special thanks
to Rachel Elliot
and Fiona Munro

Reading Consultant: Prue Goodwin, lecturer in literacy and children's books.

ORCHARD BOOKS

This story first published in Great Britain in 2009 by Orchard Books
First published as an Early Reader in 2014
This edition published in 2019 by The Watts Publishing Group

1 3 5 7 9 10 8 6 4 2

HiT entertainment

A CIP catalogue record for this book is available from the British Library.

ISBN 978 1 40835 984 6

Printed in China

MIX
Paper from
responsible sources
FSC® C104740
FSC
www.fsc.org

The paper and board used in this book are made from wood from responsible sources

Orchard Books
An imprint of Hachette Children's Group
Part of The Watts Publishing Group Limited
Carmelite House, 50 Victoria Embankment, London EC4Y 0DZ

An Hachette UK Company
www.hachette.co.uk
www.hachettechildrens.co.uk

Destiny the Pop Star Fairy was originally published
as a Rainbow Magic special. This version has
been specially adapted for developing readers
in conjunction with a Reading Consultant.